I Love You Already!

By Jory John

Illustrated by Benji Davies

HARPER
An Imprint of HarperCollinsPublishers

I Love You Already!
Text copyright © 2016 by Jory John
Illustrations copyright © 2016 by Benji Davies
All rights reserved. Printed in the United States of America.

ISBN: 978-0-06-237095-2
Typography by Jeanne L. Hogle
16 17 18 19 PC 10 9 8 7 6 5 4 3 2
❖
First Edition

This book is dedicated to
my great friend, Bill Olin.
—Jory John

For my one true love, Nina
—Benji Davies

"Ahh, I really love spending lazy weekend mornings around my house."

"A morning stroll would be nice. I wonder what ol' Bear is up to."

"Ahhhhhh. Perfect. I have everything I need to spend a pleasant day by myself."

"Bear! It's *Duck*! From next door!
Open up! C'mon, buddy!"

"**What is it, Duck?
I'm busy.**"

"You don't *look* busy! Besides, we're going for a walk, friend. No arguments. Chop-chop!"

"We can spend some
quality time together."

"No."

"I'll tell you my life's story."

"No."

"You'll tell me *your* life's
story?"

"No."

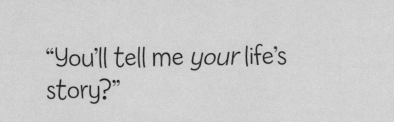

"We'll get some exercise."

"No."

"We'll look at the clouds."

"No."

"I'll tell you my life's story."

"You already said that."

"But maybe you'll *like* me more...."

"I like you *already*, Duck."

"I'm not taking no for an answer, Bear. We're having fun, whether you want to or not."

"Ugh."

"The absolute best morning you've ever had?"

"No."

"Pleasant?"

"You already said that."

"I just want you to like me, Bear."

"I LIKE YOU ALREADY!"

"But I also like quiet time *by myself.*

If you need me, I'll be relaxing by that tree.

"Now *this* is pleasant. Yes."

"Psst! Bear!!"

"**Duck! *Duck!* Are you okay?**"

"Why do *you* care?"

"**What do you mean? You're my best friend, Duck!**"

"You sure don't act like it."

"You're like my brother."

"Yeah, right."

"I should've caught you."

"I agree."

"You don't even like me, do you, Bear?"

**"Nonsense. You're basically my family.
I *love* you already, Duck!"**

"Really?
You mean it, Bear?
Do you?
You do?
Huh?"

(Sigh.) **"Yes."**

"That's such good news, Bear!
Now we can go on morning
walks together, *every single
day*! How fun! How perfect!
Especially because we live
right next door to each
other. I always know
where to find you!"

"Oh . . . great."

"So . . . you want to see me run really fast, Bear?"

"No."

"Juggle five apples?"

"No."

"Swim across this lake?"

"No."

"See you tomorrow, Bear! Bright and early. I love you already *too*, ol' chum."

"I've *got* to stop answering my door."